MW00907622

Australia

Where Koalas
Live in
Australia

For James,
No matter where life takes us,
I'll always boomerang back home to you.
—CH

For the illustrators
of the SCBWI Midsouth chapter,
for all the education, critiques, and feedback.
—BB

Koala Crossing was published by San Diego Zoo Wildlife Alliance Press in association with Blue Sneaker Press. Through these publishing efforts, we seek to inspire children and adults to care about wildlife, the natural world, and conservation.

San Diego Zoo Wildlife Alliance is a nonprofit conservation organization that is committed to saving species worldwide by uniting its expertise in animal care and conservation science with its dedication to inspiring a passion for nature. Its vision is a world where all life thrives.

Paul Baribault, President and Chief Executive Officer
Shawn Dixon, Chief Operating Officer
David Miller, Chief Marketing Officer
Georgeanne Irvine, Director of Publishing

San Diego Zoo Wildlife Alliance
P.O. Box 120551
San Diego, CA 92112-0551
sdzwa.org | 619-231-1515

San Diego Zoo Wildlife Alliance's publishing partner is Blue Sneaker Press,
an imprint of Southwestern Publishing House, Inc., 2451 Atrium Way, Nashville, TN 37214.

Southwestern Publishing House is a wholly owned subsidiary of Southwestern Family of Companies, Nashville, Tennessee.

Southwestern Publishing House, Inc.
swpublishinghouse.com | 800-358-0560

Christopher G. Capen, President
Kristin Connelly, Managing Editor
Steve Newman, Art Director

Text and illustrations copyright ©2022 San Diego Zoo Wildlife Alliance

All rights reserved. No part of this book may be reproduced or transmitted in any form or by any means, electronic or mechanical, including photocopying or recording, or by any information retrieval system, without the written permission of the copyright holder.

ISBN: 978-1-943198-15-3 | Library of Congress Control Number: 2021909999
Printed in China | 10 9 8 7 6 5 4 3 2 1

In the Land Down Under, a grove of eucalyptus trees stretched high into the bright blue Australian sky. And, in a crook of the very tallest tree, a koala was wedged between two branches.

But there wasn't just one koala. There were two—a mother named Mahmi and her joey named Garbaa.

Usually, the koala pair spent their days munching on eucalyptus leaves from their favorite tree and taking long naps. And after napping, they would munch some more before snoozing once again.

Normally, the koalas could get all the water they needed from the eucalyptus leaves. But today was different. It was hot. Very hot. The koalas were too hot and too thirsty to sleep.

"Let's go down to the stream," Mahmi suggested. A drink and a splash were just what they needed.

After a long drink Garbaa asked, "Can we rest here?"

"That's a good idea," Mahmi replied. "We'll head back home after our nap."

"Mama, why did you name me Garbaa?" the joey asked before they went to sleep.

"Well," Mahmi replied, "Garbaa means 'boomerang.' I hope that wherever you go, you'll always come back."

"Just like a boomerang," Garbaa said.

"That's right," Mahmi answered with a smile and a cuddle. "Just like a boomerang."

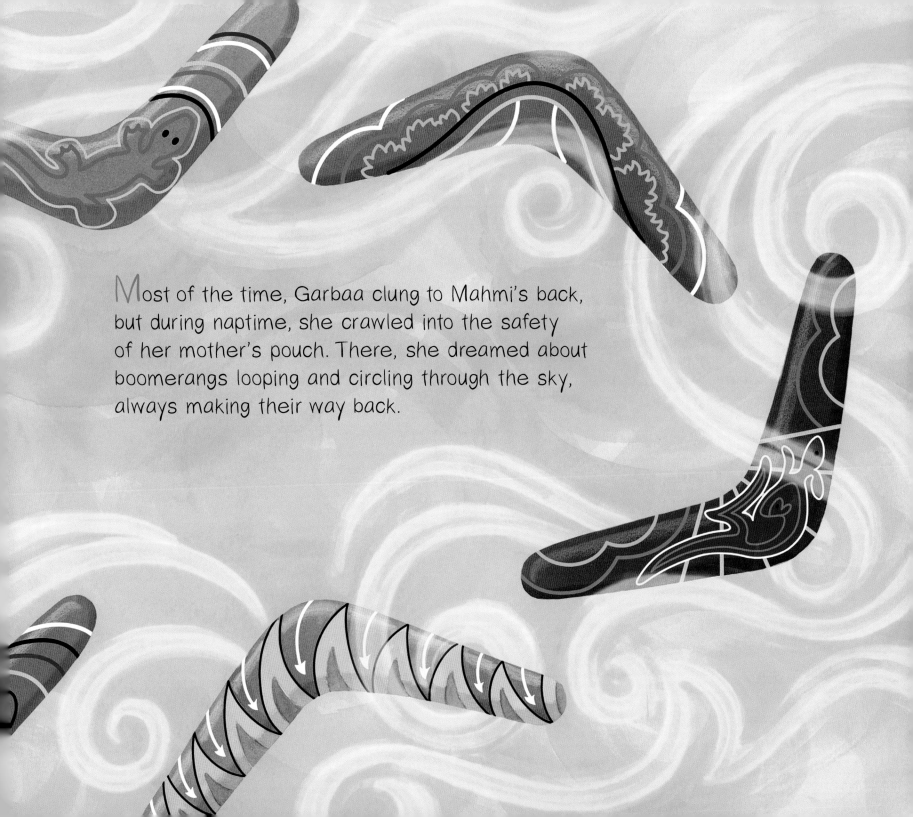

Most of the time, Garbaa clung to Mahmi's back, but during naptime, she crawled into the safety of her mother's pouch. There, she dreamed about boomerangs looping and circling through the sky, always making their way back.

A few hours later, Garbaa and Mahmi woke to a terrible crashing and screeching, sawing and thumping. Below them, they could see a swath of dirt and rocks slashing a line where trees used to stand. A road was being built.

Their favorite tree was still standing, but it was on the other side.

"How will we get back home?" the joey asked, worried.

"Maybe we can cross the road," Mahmi replied.

But when they reached the side of the road, large and loud machines rumbled and rolled past them. It was too dangerous.

Mahmi sat down to think when, suddenly, they heard an unexpected greeting.

"G'day, mates!" Muluny the platypus had seen the koalas while searching for a snack.

"Do you know where we can cross the road?" Mahmi asked.

"I know the way. Follow me!" Muluny answered. With a flick of his round tail, he led the two down to the stream that flowed alongside the road.

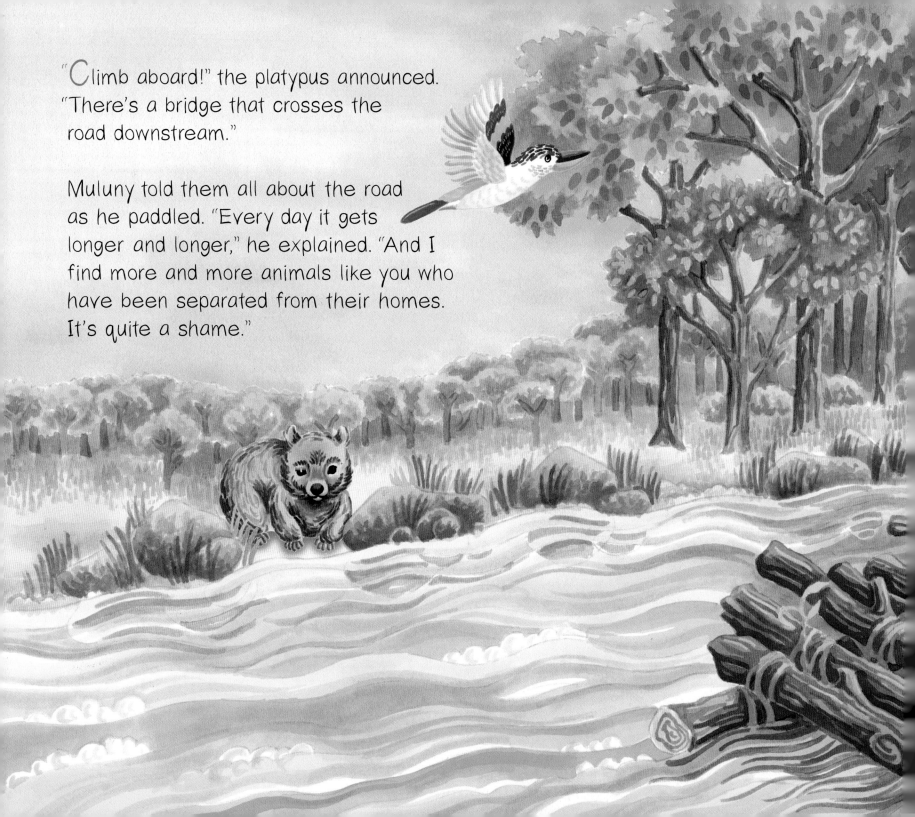

"Climb aboard!" the platypus announced. "There's a bridge that crosses the road downstream."

Muluny told them all about the road as he paddled. "Every day it gets longer and longer," he explained. "And I find more and more animals like you who have been separated from their homes. It's quite a shame."

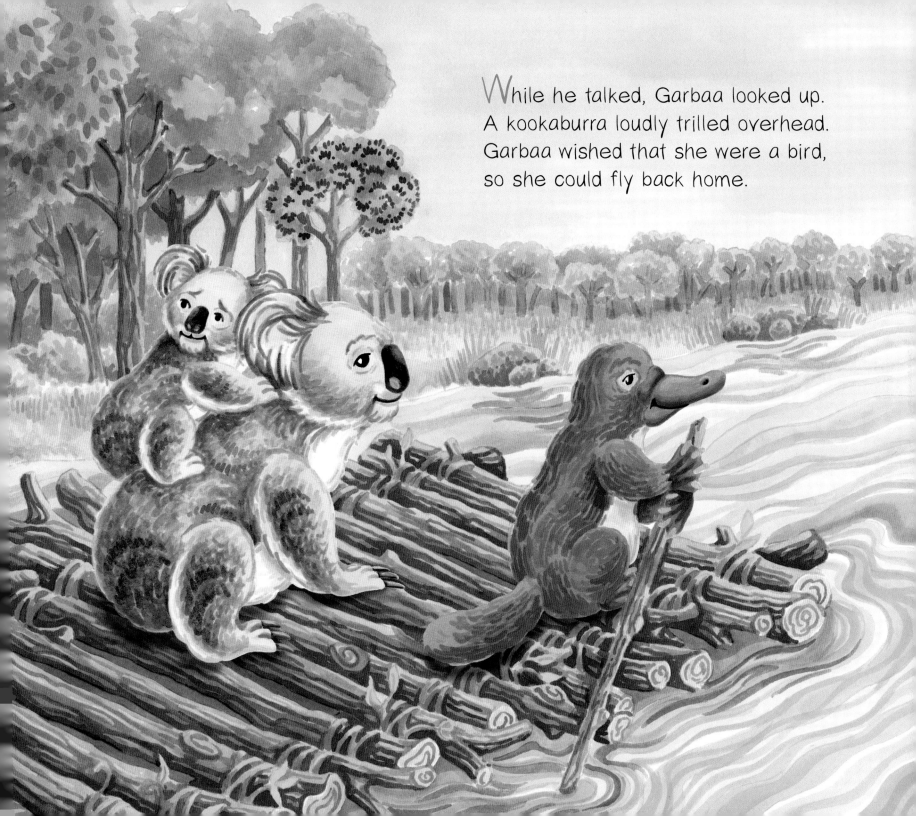

While he talked, Garbaa looked up. A kookaburra loudly trilled overhead. Garbaa wished that she were a bird, so she could fly back home.

After a long while, the platypus finally pulled the raft to the side of the stream. "Here we are! It's just up ahead. Good luck, mates!"

But the koalas couldn't see anything through the trees. And, they were still on the wrong side of the road.

"We'll be home soon," Mahmi assured her joey, but she wasn't so sure herself.

Garbaa and Mahmi climbed a tree for a better view.

"Look!" Garbaa pointed across the treetops.

From their spot up in the tree, they could see a bridge covered in grass and brush. Saplings were beginning to grow.

"Helloooooo up there!" a
kangaroo called to them from down
below. "I'm here to show you the way."

But when Mahmi and Garbaa reached
the ground, they noticed there wasn't
just one kangaroo. There were two—
the kangaroo and her joey.

Surprised, the two joeys peered at
one another. They didn't know there
was more than one kind of joey.

"Come on now," the kangaroo encouraged. "It's just a hop, skip, and jump away."

When they got to the bridge, Mahmi and Garbaa realized it wasn't just a bridge, it was a *crossing*. A koala crossing. But, not just for koalas. Koalas and kangaroos, wallabies and sugar gliders—animals near and far used the bridge to connect their worlds.

Mahmi and Garbaa smiled knowing they would be home soon.

WILDLIFE XING

Back in the safety of their home tree, Mahmi and Garbaa climbed to a high crook. Down below they could see the road. New saplings were being planted to replace some of the trees that had been cut down. And in the distance, they spotted the wildlife crossing.

"We made it back home," Mahmi announced.

"Just like a boomerang!" Garbaa replied.

"Yes," Mahmi said with a smile and a cuddle. "Just like a boomerang."

Save the Koalas!

With fuzzy ears and furry bodies, koalas are some of the most beloved animals around the world. Koalas, native to Australia, are harmless to humans and spend most of their time eating and sleeping. But, these adorable creatures need our help!

Habitat loss poses the biggest threat to koalas' survival:

- Trees are being cut down and land is being cleared to make space for roads, homes, and ranches.
- Without eucalyptus trees, koalas don't have a safe home or a source of food.
- Some koalas are being run over by cars.
- Because of climate change, devastating bushfires are more frequent. Buhfires in late 2019 and early 2020 killed an estimated 1.25 billion animals, including thousands of koalas, and destroyed more than 27.2 million acres of habitat.
- Roads and cleared land create cut-off, isolated pockets of koala populations.

But there is hope!

It's not too late to help save the koalas:

- San Diego Zoo Wildlife Alliance's conservation partners are studying wild koala populations to learn more about their behavior and ways to save them.
- Laws, such as the Koala Protection Act, are being considered to help protect koala habitat.
- Wildlife crossings are being built to keep habitats intact, allowing animals to migrate, search for food, and stay connected.

Holger Detje

Gary Runn

Darryl Jones

The Compton Road wildlife crossing in Brisbane, Australia, allows animals, such as koalas, kangaroos, sugar gliders, and wombats, to safely cross the road.

nyker/Shutterstock.com

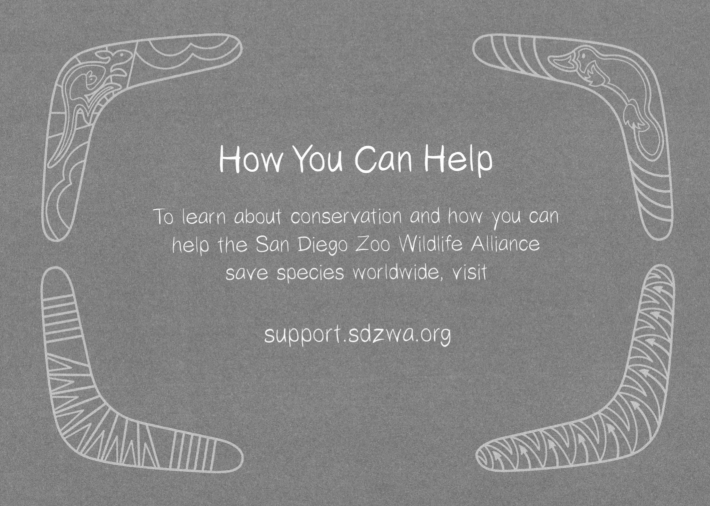

How You Can Help

To learn about conservation and how you can
help the San Diego Zoo Wildlife Alliance
save species worldwide, visit

support.sdzwa.org

Our appreciation and gratitude to Aboriginal Cultural Consultant
Sam Cook (Nyikina Nation) for her review of *Koala Crossing*.

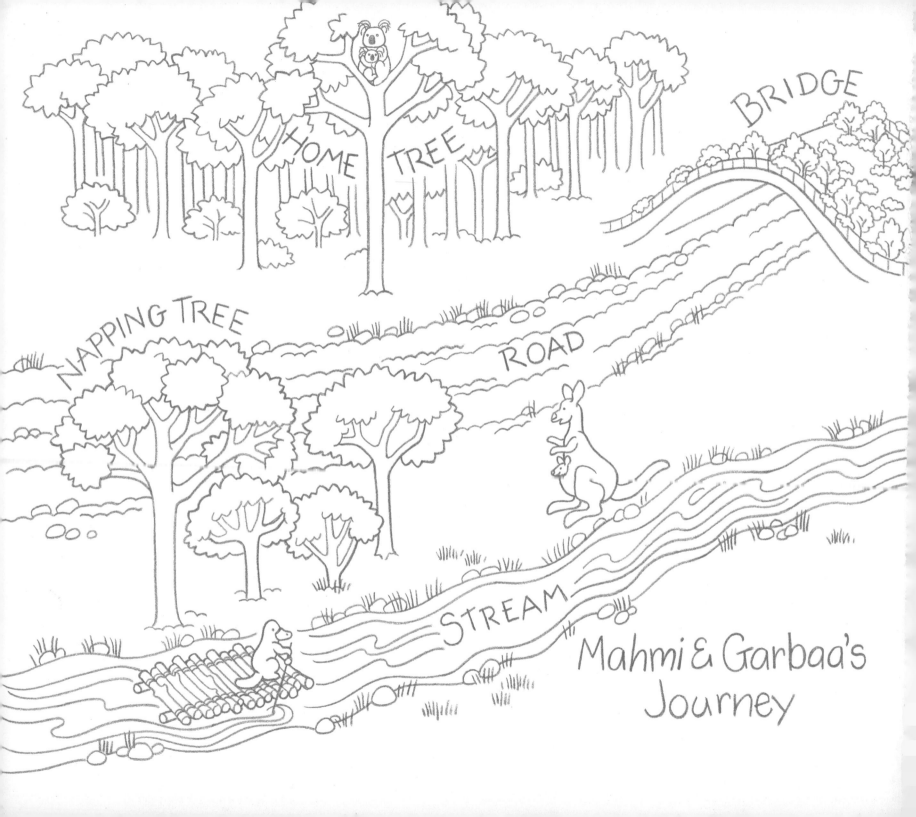

HOME TREE

BRIDGE

NAPPING TREE

ROAD

STREAM

Mahmi & Garbaa's Journey